#Help! Study Hacks

How Do I Give a Great Speech?

Sarah Eason and
Louise Spilsbury

CHERITON
CHILDREN'S BOOKS

Please visit our website, www.cheritonchildrensbooks.com to see more of our high-quality books.

First Edition

Published in 2022 by **Cheriton Children's Books**
PO Box 7258, Bridgnorth WV16 9ET, UK

Authors: Sarah Eason and Louise Spilsbury
Designer: Paul Myerscough
Editor: Jennifer Sanderson
Picture Researcher: Rachel Blount
Proofreader: Wendy Scavuzzo

Picture credits: Cover: Shutterstock/VaLiza. Inside: p1: Shutterstock/Wavebreakmedia; p4: Shutterstock/Robert Kneschke; p5: Shutterstock/Monkey Business Images; p6: Shutterstock/Potstock; p7: Shutterstock/Lightpoet; p8: Shutterstock/Wavebreakmedia; p9: Shutterstock/stockphoto-graf; p10: Shutterstock/Rawpixel.com; p11: Shutterstock/Javier Brosch; p12: Shutterstock/Odua Images; p13: Shutterstock/Valery Sidelnykov; p14: Shutterstock/Elena Eryomenko; p15: Shutterstock/Syda Productions; p16: Shutterstock/insta_photos; p17: Shutterstock/Monkey Business Images; p18: Shutterstock/insta_photos; p19: Shutterstock/ViDI Studio; p20: Shutterstock; p21: Shutterstock/Roman Samborskyi; p22: Shutterstock; p23: Shutterstock/RapunzielStock; p24: Shutterstock/Dragon Images; p25: Shutterstock/myboys.me; p26: Shutterstock/Syda Productions; p27: Shutterstock/Gorodenkoff; p28: Shutterstock/Dmytro Zinkevych; p29: Shutterstock/Wavebreakmedia.

Printed in the United States of America

Contents

Introduction

Help! How Do I Give a Great Speech?

#Help! Your teacher has asked you to **present** your project in class next week—and you've never spoken in public before. #TotallyFreakingOut! Hey, relax and take a breath, because help is at hand! Anyone can learn to give a great speech or **presentation**. And once you know how to do it well, it can be really fun, too! So let's learn how.

Public Speaking—What's So Great?

To be able to speak clearly to other people is a great skill to have—not just for school, but for life. Public speaking is a part of many jobs, such as being a lawyer, manager, actor, or a teacher. And it's not just at school or work that being able to speak in public is important. Being able to make people listen to you in your personal life is important, too. If you can speak well, you can **communicate** well with your family and friends. And that helps stop a lot of arguments!

Once you know how to speak in public, giving a class presentation will be fun.

Good communication skills are important in all areas of your life.

Freaking Out About Speaking Out

If you feel nervous about giving a speech or talking in front of classmates, don't worry—it's normal. Everyone feels a little anxious about speaking in public, but once you start to practice it, it gets a whole lot easier. And if you get used to it now, while you are young, you'll find it a cinch when you are grown up. When you feel nervous about speaking in public, just remember why learning to do it is so great:

- It helps you feel confident and builds great **self-esteem**.
- It teaches you how to organize your ideas.
- It helps you communicate information in a confident way.
- It makes you feel really proud of yourself afterward!

#Help!

Where Do I Start?

Like all useful skills, learning to speak in front of others takes time—it doesn't happen by magic. You can learn public speaking skills step by step, just like any other task.

Chapter One

Help! How Do I Put a Speech Together?

#TotallyTongue-Tied! Do you get nervous about public speaking because you worry that the words just won't come out? This happens to a lot of people—they get scared that they will get tongue-tied as soon as they open their mouth. The way to get over this is to practice, practice, practice. The more you speak up in front of a group of people, the easier it will get. Promise!

#Hack: Practice speaking in front of people by telling your parents what you did at school.

You Can Hack It!

Try watching people talking in public. Do you notice any tricks that they use to get their points across? What are these?

Starting Out Made Easy

To ease yourself into speaking out, start off at home. Get into the habit of talking to your parents about your school day—every day. If you have younger brothers or sisters, try reading them a story. If you have grandparents, ask them to listen while you speak out loud to them.

Bring the Drama!

If you like drama, it's a great way to get into public speaking. For example, you could put on a short play for your classmates or family. Most schools or communities run drama clubs that you can join, so why not check out what's available near to where you live? Taking part in a show or play helps you learn things such as **projecting** your voice so that an audience can hear it. Performing regularly in public will help you get over any nerves about speaking out, too. You'll also get to listen to other public speakers, which will help you learn how to improve your own public speaking.

#Help!

How Do I Test My Skills?

Here's a quick guide to testing out your public speaking skills at home:

- First, ask a parent to suggest a **topic** for you to speak about.
- Do not look at any books or notes to help you! You need to speak up with your own words.
- Just talk for 30 seconds about the topic. It doesn't matter what you say, as long as you keep on speaking!

What Will I Say?

Have you ever seen your teacher stand up in front of the class and say, "I forgot to plan my class last night, so I'm just going to wing it today?!" Probably not! Anyone who regularly speaks in public knows that they need to plan what they are going to say. So, if you need to give a speech, you need to plan ahead, too.

#Hack: The library is a great place to **research** facts. Why not ask your school librarian to help you get started?

Keep It Interesting

If you are allowed to choose your speech topic, try to choose one that you like and are interested in. You'll enjoy working on it more, and chances are you will feel more confident talking about it, too. Try to choose something you know a lot about and are comfortable talking about, such as your favorite sport or what you like to do on weekends.

Back It Up!

How do you know what you want to say? Well, the best speeches are packed with facts and **evidence**. They can back up **opinions** that you give in **debates** and explain **statements** in a presentation. You can research facts from websites, library books, **encyclopedias**, newspapers, and magazines. You can also use your community for research, such as interviewing local people, family, and friends.

#Help!

How Do I Come Up with Ideas?

If you are struggling to come up with a topic for your speech, try **brainstorming**. Here's how:

- For five minutes, write down what interests you or what you like doing. Don't stop writing, just keep going for the whole time.
- Ask your friends to help if you feel you need some more ideas—repeat the five minutes with their help.
- Look at your list of topics, then choose the one you like the most and think you can best talk about.

Keep It Clear

Choosing a main topic is one thing but, when you have to give a long talk, it's good to divide your material into **subtopics**. So, for example, if you have to give a talk about **habitats**, you might start with a general explanation of what a habitat is and then have subtopics on ocean habitats, **grassland** habitats, mountain habitats, and so on. Grouping information in a clear way makes it easier to write a speech—and easier for people to follow it.

If you are giving a talk about tropical reefs, you could break your topic into subjects such as plants and animals.

Who Do You Think You're Talking To?

Writing with your audience in mind turns a good speech into a great speech. When you are planning what to say, spend time thinking about what the audience would like to hear in your speech. Try to also figure out what they are likely to be interested in, and what will keep them listening.

What's the Point?

Always keep in mind the main **purpose** of your speech. Different speeches have different jobs to do. Some speeches are simply meant to **inform** the audience, such as when a teacher asks you to speak about healthy eating or the dangers of smoking. Some speeches are meant to be persuasive. That means your speech has to persuade the audience to agree with you or vote for you. Other speeches need to be more entertaining, for example, when you accept an award and want to include a joke.

If your audience is full of young children, make sure you choose a topic that will interest them, such as popular books or television characters.

Target Your Audience

Knowing your audience can help you plan and write your speech. Here are some things to consider when you are planning:

- Is the speech right for the age of your audience? For example, if you're talking to younger children, use simple ideas and **vocabulary**.
- Will your topic be interesting to the audience? For example, if you're talking to an audience of football players, don't talk about tennis!
- How much does your audience already know about the topic? Try to tell them something new, not something they already know.

#Help!

How Do I Keep Them Interested?

Try to think of fun and interesting ways to keep your **target audience** listening. First, think of what interests them. Then, think about how you could link to those interests in your speech. Could you use a funny story, for example, or a joke?

How Do I Write a Great Speech?

Would you head off on vacation without knowing where you are going? No! Well, you shouldn't start a speech like that either! All speeches need a **structure** that includes an introduction, a middle, and an ending. Before you start writing a speech, it helps to write an **outline** that shows what you will include in each part of your talk.

Start Off Strong

The introduction is the beginning of your speech. In it, you tell the audience what the speech is about and what main areas you will be covering. The best introductions are quite short, but get the audience's attention. They include something interesting or fun that hooks people in. Your introduction should also tell the audience why your speech will be important or interesting.

It's worth taking the time to plan your outline carefully. It will give you a clear structure to follow throughout your speech.

Can I Draw an Outline?

Yes, absolutely! Diagrams such as mindmaps and flowcharts are great ways to get your ideas onto paper and help you start shaping your outline. Make a rough version to start with, and polish it up later.

#Help!

Max the Middle

In the middle or main part of your speech, talk about the subtopics you uncovered while researching the topic. Divide it into paragraphs, with a separate paragraph for each new subtopic. If there is a time limit for your speech, figure out how many paragraphs you can include. Start each with a sentence that really grabs the audience's attention.

Amazing Endings

The end of your speech is the conclusion. Most speakers use the conclusion to remind listeners of the most important things they said in their speech. Like introductions, the best conclusions are brief but memorable. Try to remember the last sentence of your conclusion, so you can look at your audience when you say it. Make it snappy so the audience remembers it.

You Can Hack It!

Plagiarism is using someone else's words and passing them off as your own. How might your audience react if they found out your speech includes plagiarism? Why do you think it is important to write using your own words?

Chapter Two

Help! How Do I Present Well?

#AllEyesOnMe! Did you know that there are tools that you can use to get and keep your audience's attention? For example, have you ever seen a person give a speech while using **props**? Perhaps they used a puppet? Maybe they wrote on a whiteboard? They may even have used a pet! These are all visual aids. They help get the audience's attention and help you explain what you are talking about. They also give you something to do with your hands—other than stuffing them in your pockets!

Presentation? Put a Prop in It!

There are a lot of ways that visual aids can help your speech or presentation. Here are a few ideas to try:

- Are parts of your speech complicated? If so, try pointing to items on posters or **overheads** to help the audience understand what you are saying.

Props can help explain ideas. For example, if you are talking about healthy eating, you could use a photo that shows good food choices.

Try to use your props appropriately. For example, a fun costume works for a talk about Halloween, but not when talking about serious issues.

- If you show photos, illustrations, or videos of something such as a tornado, it will be more **effective** than trying to describe it with words alone.
- Why not show facts and figures with pie charts, graphs, or diagrams? This is far more interesting than reading them aloud.

How to Use Props Like a Pro

There are some important things to remember when using props and visual aids.

- Use props to highlight important points, not just for the sake of using them. They should really add something to the speech.
- Be sure that everyone in your audience can see any visual aids or props you use—even right at the back. They are no good if people cannot see them!
- Be sure equipment is easy to use. Fiddling with buttons or displays during the speech will **distract** your audience.
- Keep it practical. Bringing in an animal might make a talk more realistic, but it could go horribly wrong ... !

#Help!

What If It All Goes Wrong?

Using props doesn't always work out! If the equipment you are planning to use fails, have some printed sheets to hand out in case your computer doesn't work or the video equipment you need isn't available.

How Do I Use Body Language?

Did you know that when someone speaks to us, we don't listen just to their words? That's right—about 70 percent of human communication is **nonverbal**. That means people say more through the way they stand, how they hold their arms, and their **facial expressions** than they ever say in words! Who knew our bodies have so much to say!

Heads Up!

Your posture, or the way you hold your body, can help you look interested and confident. And that makes people more likely to pay attention to what you are saying. When you are giving a speech, try to remember these top tips for great posture:

- Stand straight and tall.
- Avoid slouching or shuffling from one foot to the other.
- Try not to fiddle with your hands, clothes, or hair.
- Never turn your side or back to the audience.
- Don't walk back and forth too much—that could distract your listeners.

A confident speaker is more interesting to listen to, whether that is in person or on a screen.

Look Me in the Eye!

Making eye contact with your audience, or looking them in the eye, can help keep them interested in what you are saying. Try to look directly at them, rather than looking at your feet or staring at a spot on the wall. Some speakers like to look into the eyes of as many audience members as they can while they speak in order to get and keep their attention. That makes everyone in the room feel that they have your attention and that your speech is directed at them.

#Hack: If you find that you fiddle with your hands, hold them behind your back while you talk.

#Help!

How Do I Use Gestures?

You can bring life to your presentation with **gestures**, too. For example, you can use your hands to show how big something is or to **emphasize** a number, such as "There are three things you need to remember about this..." Here are some great ways to make the best use of gestures:

- Only use gestures that you would normally use in conversation.
- Try not to use gestures you are not familiar with—you'll just feel awkward.
- Match your facial expressions to your words. Smile if your speech is funny or has a positive message. Look **sincere** if the theme is more serious.

How Do I Remember What to Say?

So, how do you learn your speech? Well, the good news is that you don't have to learn the whole thing by heart! If you just spoke it aloud word for word, it would sound pretty boring. However, it is useful to try to remember the key points of your speech. The best way to do that is to write notes on **index cards**. You'll be able to keep checking them as you talk. That will keep your speech on track, while making it sound natural, too.

Keep to Key Points

You can buy index cards or cut pieces of paper or cardboard small enough to hold in your hand easily. Pick out the main points of your speech and write key words or a few notes about each of those points on separate cards. Number the cards in case they get mixed up and out of order. For example, if you're giving a talk about food chains, you might use key words such as "plants," "make own food," "herbivores such as zebras," "carnivores such as lions." Then you can glance at these words to jog your memory during your presentation.

If you make a recording of yourself giving a presentation or speech, it will help you remember it. You can also use it to work on improving your presentation.

#Hack: Practice any gestures as you practice your speech. It will help you remember the words.

#Help!

How Can I Remember?

Here are some things you can do to help you remember important parts of your speech.

- When you learn a section of a speech, decide exactly which gestures you want to use. Then, practice them.
- Copy the speech, or sections of it, onto a sheet of paper. Read the words aloud to yourself as you write. That can help your brain remember them.
- If you have made a recording of yourself reading the speech, listen to it as often as you can and try to speak along with it. Constant repetition helps us remember things.
- Go to sleep soon after you have learned a section of your speech. It is one of the best ways of helping your brain remember it.

How Do I Make Myself Clear?

Imagine you are listening to two speakers. One has a confident voice. The other mutters their words, and is fidgety and nervous. Who would you find more convincing? The speaker with the confident voice, right? If you speak with confidence, and **pronounce** your words clearly, people will listen to you.

Don't Be a Phony!

When you make a speech, don't put on a fake voice. Try to sound like yourself and use a natural voice. Use words that are familiar to you, unless you're explaining something scientific or technical. Another way to sound more natural is to use **pauses** and **stresses**. When we speak normally, we pause between **phrases** or stress key words to emphasize their meaning, for example, "You'll never guess what happened next... (pause). She told me she ate the ENTIRE birthday cake!"

You Can Hack It!

Can you think of people you know who speak clearly? What do they do during their presentations to help get across their viewpoints?

#Help!

How Do I Speak Clearly?

When you're practicing a speech, remember these tips:

- Speak at a medium **pace**—not too fast or too slow. Lots of people talk faster when they are nervous, so take your time.
- Pronounce your words clearly, and don't **slur** them. Make sure you say the ends of words, especially the d's, t's, and ing's at the ends of words.
- Don't overuse sounds such as "Um" and "Uh," or words such as "you know" to fill spaces in your speech. They make you sound unprepared.
- Keep your index cards nearby and stay **focused** so you don't need to use filler words.

Try Out a Tongue Twister

Tongue twisters are not just for fun! To reduce their chances of tripping over their words during a speech, or losing their place, some people practice tongue twisters. Tongue twisters exercise the face, lip, and tongue muscles we use when we speak.

Try this fun tongue twister: She sells seashells by the seashore!

How Do I Polish My Speech?

Have you heard the saying "practice makes perfect?" It's the sort of thing that your mom would say to you, but it really is true! If you practice your speech or presentation a lot before you do it for real, you will **deliver** it in style. You'll be familiar and comfortable with what you are saying. That will make you feel confident, and your speech will seem really polished.

It's All About the Timing

When you practice your speech and you feel you are speaking at a comfortable pace, not too quickly or too slowly, use a clock or a stopwatch to time it. That way, you can pace your speech to fit the time you have been given.

Even people who do a lot of public speaking rely on preparation and practice to make better speeches.

#Hack: Don't forget to use your props when you practice.

Fake It Till You Make It

You may not feel confident about public speaking but, if you practice looking more confident, you will soon feel it for real. The idea is to fake it till you make it! If you can speak calmly and clearly, and remember the tips about body language, the audience won't be able to tell that you feel nervous inside. You'll get the chance to overcome your fear through practice. Making sure you practice your talk many times beforehand helps you appear more confident, too. Even if you're nervous, you will know roughly what you should say, so you can keep going no matter what.

#Help!

How Do I Practice?

Practicing a speech or presentation is a great skill to master. Try using these key stages to become a pro at practice:

- Read your speech alone in front of a mirror until you feel more confident.
- Do it for someone you feel comfortable with, such as a parent or friend. Ask them to stand back so they can tell if you are speaking loudly enough.
- Record yourself so you can watch it.
- Give and get **feedback**. Ask yourself and others what could be improved in terms of the information you have included and how you presented it.

Chapter Three

Help! How Do I Control My Feelings?

#GetMeOuttaHere!
Do you get butterflies in your stomach before a speech or presentation? Don't worry—it happens to pretty much everyone! Even the most experienced public speakers get nervous from time to time. A little nervous energy can be a good thing, though, because it helps you perform well. And there are a lot of things you can do to stop you from getting too nervous.

#Hack: Keep your headphones with you so you can listen to some music to keep you calm before giving your speech.

It's Time to Warm Up!

Many performers and public speakers have certain things they always do to get themselves warmed up before going on. Some put on their headphones and listen to their favorite song. Others get a **pep talk** from a friend. Others repeat a few **inspiring** words to themselves, such as "You can do it!" over and over.

#Help!

How Do I Calm Down?

Try this breathing exercise to free up your lungs to allow you to speak loudly and clearly. It will also help you feel calmer and better prepared to speak.

- Close your mouth and breathe in deeply through your nose.
- Hold this breath for five seconds.
- Then, breathe out slowly through your mouth.
- Keep doing this until you feel calmer.
- Listening to music can relax you before a public speech.

See Your Success

How good will you feel when you finish your speech and know you've done it to the best of your ability? Before you get ready to give a speech, spend a minute or two imagining that feeling. In your mind, watch a movie of yourself making your speech just as well as, if not better than, all the times you've practiced it. Imagine smiling confidently, listening to the applause, and seeing your teacher nod with approval. Then take that feeling into the speech with you.

It feels good when your parents or guardians tell you how great you did! Keep that good feeling with you during your speech.

How Do I Listen to a Speech?

Did you know that, to be a great speaker, you need to be a great listener? That's right—if you can listen well to other people, it will help you learn how to speak well. If you treat what other people say as important, they will listen to you more respectfully, too. And knowing how to give helpful feedback on other people's presentations can help your own.

Be a Great Listener

Listening well is as much a skill as talking well. Follow these top tips to make sure you listen to others when they speak in public:

- *Pay attention.* Try not to fidget, stare out the window, or talk to your neighbor. If you're distracted, it's hard for the speaker to concentrate, and you will lose the thread of the talk.
- *Value the speaker.* What you have to say is important, isn't it? You want other people to value it, don't you? That's why you should value what other people have to say, too.

You Can Hack It!

When listening to other people speaking in private or in public, remember this important rule: Treat other people the way you would like to be treated. What behavior would you find upsetting if you were trying to give a speech?

Try to always be polite when you ask a speaker a question.

- *Show your appreciation*. Make sure that you always applaud others for their efforts when they speak in public.
- *Be kind*. Most people get a little nervous, so never laugh at or make fun of a speaker.

#Help!

How Do I Give Feedback?

It is good to know how to ask questions about something you have just heard because that helps you learn to field questions from an audience. Follow these steps to make sure you ask questions and give feedback politely:

- If you are allowed to ask questions after someone has spoken, always hold your hand up.
- Everyone has differing abilities, so be aware of other people's feelings. Some people won't be able to produce as complicated a presentation as others. Remember that it is their effort that counts.
- Provide feedback in a positive way. Don't be rude or hurtful.

Conclusion

Help! How Do I Give a Great Speech—Forever?

#TimeToTalk! It's the day of your speech or presentation. You've done your research, planned your talk, written your index cards, practiced the words, and rehearsed with the visual aids. Then, it's time to give your speech—and you wow the crowd! So, what's next?

And finally—when it is time for you to speak, don't forget to enjoy it!

Make Your Speeches Even Better

Keep working on your public speaking skills, and think about how you could improve. For example, why not speak directly to your listeners and ask them what they think about the topic you've been discussing? Or you could encourage them to take action—for example, if you have been talking about the importance of exercise, you could suggest that they take up a new sport. And never forget to polish your endings. After all, that is the part of your speech your audience is most likely to remember.

#Help!

How Do I Check How I Did?

After you make a presentation or speech, think back to how it went. Ask yourself some questions, like these:

- How did it feel to speak in front of a group?
- Did people respond as though they could hear everything?
- Did you keep the audience's interest?
- What could you have done better?
- When do you think you might speak in public again?

Speak Up for Life!

Now that you've learned how to be a great public speaker, keep on working on this amazing skill for the rest of your life. Speaking in public isn't just about giving a speech or a presentation. It's about making your opinions heard. It's about getting others to understand what you think and feel. It's about engaging and communicating with other people. These are all really important tools that you will need in your everyday life, forever.

When a speech goes well, soak up the applause that comes your way!

Glossary

brainstorming solving a problem by thinking intensely about it
communicate the exchange of information with other people
debates arguments in which people put forward different opinions
deliver to produce or put forward
distract to draw someone's attention away from something
effective bringing about a good result
emphasize to draw attention to something
encyclopedias books that provide information about many subjects
engaged focused and interested in
evidence facts and information that support things that people write or say
facial expressions movements of the face that show a person's emotions
feedback response to information
focused concentrating on something
gestures movements that a person makes with their hands to help them explain what they are saying
grassland a habitat made up of mainly grasses with some trees and shrubs
habitats places in which organisms live, such as grasslands or oceans
index cards small lined cards for note-making
inform to tell somebody something
inspiring making people want to do something
nonverbal without spoken words
opinions people's ideas and beliefs about something
outline a written general plan that shows the main features of something
overheads devices that project words and images onto a screen
pace the speed at which something moves
pauses temporary stops in action or speech
pep talk an encouraging talk to help a person feel confident
phrases groups of words that convey, or show, an idea
present to show or put forward something
presentation a sharing of a person's work or ideas
projecting throwing forward
pronounce to use the voice to make certain sounds or say words correctly
props objects used during a performance to help the audience engage with it
purpose the reason for doing something
research investigate something
self-esteem feeling proud about oneself
sincere honest and truthful
slur to say words without pronouncing them clearly
statements something stated, or said or written officially
stresses where specific words or syllables stand out more by saying them louder
structure the shape or organization of something
subtopics topics that are part of the main topic
target audience the audience at which a person's speech or presentation is aimed
topic the subject or main idea of something such as a speech
vocabulary a range of words

Find Out More

Books

Anderson, Chris. *Thank You for Coming to My TED Talk.* Clarion Books, 2020.

Harper, Leslie. *How to Give a Speech* (Be a Community Leader). PowerKids Press, 2014.

Minden, Cecilia and Kate Roth. *How to Write and Give a Speech* (Language Arts Explorer Junior). Cherry Lake Publishing, 2011.

Websites

On this website, you will find a printable template for planning a great speech and a checklist of tips:
https://planningwithkids.com/2012/10/20/public-speaking-tips-for-kids

This website gives seven brief tips on public speaking:
https://speakingschools.com.au/seven-public-speaking-tips

Although this website was written for teachers, there are lots of fun ideas for how to give an interesting speech:
www.publicspeakingforkids.org

Publisher's note to educators and parents:
All the websites featured above have been carefully reviewed to ensure that they are suitable for students. However, many websites change often, and we cannot guarantee that a site's future contents will continue to meet our high standards of educational value. Please be advised that students should be closely monitored whenever they access the Internet.

Index

About the Authors

Sarah Eason has written many children's books on a wide variety of topics. Louise Spilsbury is an award-winning author who has written hundreds of wonderful books for children. Both hope they have now learned how to give a great speech!